D0892078

Bang!
Bang!

Our Hero

Bang! Bang!

by

George Ade

[A Collection of Stories Intended to Recall Memories of the Nickel Library Days When Boys Were Supermen and Murder a Fine Art.]

Illustrated by

John T. McCutcheon

Short Story Index Reprint Series

BOOKS FOR LIBRARIES PRESS
FREEPORT, NEW YORK

First Published 1928
Reprinted 1971

INTERNATIONAL STANDARD BOOK NUMBER:
0-8369-3908-5

LIBRARY OF CONGRESS CATALOG CARD NUMBER:
75-160929

PRINTED IN THE UNITED STATES OF AMERICA

DEDICATED TO F. P. A.

These stories were first printed in the Chicago Record in the late nineties. They are boiled-down imitations of the haymow literature which was denounced by parents and encouraged by boys from the time of Horace Greeley up to the golden age ushered in by the comic strip. The nickel library came after the yellow-back novel, which dealt mostly with smoking tepees, crouching savages and trappers who were deadly with the rifle and wore fringe on their buckskin suits. One reason for the enduring popularity of the nickel library was that it could be spread open inside of a school geography and entirely concealed from any teacher who did not approach from the rear.

For the first time Eddie Parks, Cyril Smith, Clarence Allen and their brave colleagues are being put into a book. Because these narratives are a reminder of thirty years ago, they have not been revised or brought up to date. The allusions to the Spanish-American War, the Klondike, William McKinley and the League of American Wheelmen have been retained because of their historical flavor.

These stories will mean nothing to juveniles who have been pampered with roadsters and fed up on movies—who never heard of Oliver Optic, Horatio

Alger, Jr., and Jack Harkaway, to say nothing of "Shorty," "Silver Star, the Boy Knight," "Skinny, the Tin Peddler" and Frank, who invented the mechanical horse. To some of the older people they may come as a happy reminder of the days when all of us were ruined by reading books which could not be obtained at the Public Library.

THE AUTHOR.

CONTENTS

Contents

Handsome Cyril;

or,

The Messenger Boy
with the Warm Feet

SPLASH!
CYRIL
BING!
THWARTED!

HANDSOME CYRIL; or, THE MESSENGER BOY WITH THE WARM FEET

Chapter 1

The Meeting

CYRIL!"

"Alexander!"

The two messenger boys clasped hands.

It was on Madison Street—that busy thoroughfare where many streams of humanity meet in whirling vortexes.

The afternoon sun lighted up the features of Cyril Smith, the courageous young messenger boy.

His steel-gray eyes glinted as he gazed at his friend and comrade, Alexander. He had regular features and a regular suit of messenger boy clothes.

"I hope you are well, Alexander," he said, a smile lighting up his handsome face.

"Oh, yes, quite well, indeed," responded Alexander.

There was a short silence broken only by the continuous uproar of the street. Then Alexander asked: "Where are you going?"

"I am delivering a death message," replied Cyril, thoughtfully.

"Well, I must ascertain how the baseball game is progressing," said Alexander, and shaking our hero by the hand he moved away.

"Alexander is a strange youth," said Cyril, musingly. "I sometimes think he must be pessimistic."

At that moment the shriek of a woman in agony smote upon his ears.

"What is this?" he asked. "A woman in trouble? I must buy an extra and find out what has occasioned this disturbance."

For at that moment the newsboys were shouting the extras which told why the woman had screamed.

Such is life in a great city.

Our hero ran toward the corner.

Handsome Cyril

He saw a beautiful woman struggling in the grasp of a fashionably-attired man.

She was a magnificent creature. Great swirls of raven hair fell in profusion down her back. The alabaster whiteness of her face served to intensify her beauty. She wore a diamond necklace, diamond earrings, and her lily-white hands flashed with precious jewels.

She turned an appealing look at our hero and said: "Oh, sir, save me!"

Bing!

With a well-directed blow Cyril sent the fashionably-dressed man sprawling on the pavement. With the other arm he supported the fainting woman. Then with the other hand he picked up the lace handkerchief which had fallen to the ground and presented it to her with a graceful bow.

"Curse you!" shouted the villain, struggling to his feet. "I shall cause you to rue this deed."

"Coward!" exclaimed Cyril, with a curling lip. "How dare you strike this woman?"

"We shall meet again," said Cyril's antagonist, ominously, and with these words he stepped into a carriage and was driven rapidly away.

Our hero now turned his attention to the beautiful creature who reclined in his arms.

"Speak! speak!" he whispered.

Slowly the glorious eyes opened, and then she asked, in tremulous tones: "Where is he?"

"Gone."

"Where to?"

"That I cannot say, madam," responded Cyril, for though he was only a messenger boy he had been taught to be courteous.

"His name is Rudolf Belmont. He must be followed."

"Yes, madam."

"He has taken the papers which prove that I am the real owner of the Belmont estate."

A shudder passed through our hero's frame. Then recovering himself he said: "Madam, I will follow that villain and recover the papers."

"Oh, thank you," she said, and for a few minutes she wept softly.

Finally she lifted her tear-stained face and said: "Summon a conveyance and if you are ever in need of a friend come to this number," saying which she gave Cyril an engraved card and offered him a purse containing gold.

"No, madam," said Cyril, with dignity. "I will not take your money. My salary is sufficient to permit me to live in comparative luxury."

The cab which he had summoned arrived at this moment. He assisted his fair companion to enter the cab and then turned his attention to the carriage, which was by this time nearly a mile away.

"That wretch shall not escape me," he said determinedly, and without further ado he started in pursuit of the carriage, which was now a mile and a quarter away.

As he sped along the street he chanced to read the card given to him by the beautiful lady.

It ran thus:

Mrs. Gertrude Fisher
775 Michigan Boulevard
Second Flat

"Merciful heaven!" he gasped. "My mother!"

Chapter 2

TREACHERY

IT will be remembered that we left our hero pursuing the carriage containing Rudolf Belmont.

In a few moments he overtook the equipage and saw Rudolf Belmont enter a tall mansion on 12th Street.

Our hero secreted himself behind a large tree, determined to wait for an opportunity to enter the house.

An hour passed.

Cyril began to feel the pangs of hunger, but he was determined not to abandon his post.

"Ah, sir; you are a handsome youth," said some one behind him, and Cyril turned to behold a tall, handsome stranger.

Our hero acknowledged the compliment with a pleasant bow, and soon he was in conversation with the stranger.

Before departing, the stranger gave our hero a box of crackerjack, which he devoured with a relish, as it had been nearly two hours since he had tasted food.

Scarcely had he finished eating when he felt a strange faintness. Everything seemed to swim before his gaze, as though he were in a natatorium. He had to lean against the tree for support.

Suddenly the truth flashed upon him!

The crackerjack had been drugged.

The whole earth seemed enveloped in darkness. He sank to the ground.

He heard a voice, "Away with him to the basement!"

It was the voice of Rudolf Belmont!

Then all was blank!

Chapter 3

The River

WHEN our hero recovered consciousness he found himself bound and gagged and being carried along a dark thoroughfare by two rough-looking men.

He was blindfolded but he knew the men were rough-looking. They always are.

A drizzle of rain was falling and the sky overhead was inky black.

Cyril heard a voice. It was the voice of Rudolf Belmont. He was speaking to the two rough-looking men. He said: "Do your work well. Then meet me at the Rock Island depot and you shall have your money."

Cyril's heart seemed to stand still! What were they going to do?

The two ruffians carried him along a dark wall. He heard beneath him the lapping of waves. The two men spoke in muttered oaths.

He knew the horrible truth.

The river!

Our hero felt himself lifted.
Then he fell, down and down.
Splash!
The dark waters closed above him.

Chapter 4

Alexander to the Rescue

JUST as the body disappeared and the two ruffians ran back into the dark thoroughfare a boat shot across the river.

"I thought I heard something drop into the murky river," said Alexander, for it was he. "I suspect foul play."

At that instant he saw a form rise to the water's surface. He reached forth and pulled our hero into the boat. It was the work of a moment to remove the gag and ropes.

"Cyril?"

"Alexander! What are you doing here?"

"I was taking a boat ride, when I heard a sound indicating that some one had been thrown into the river. What does it mean?"

"Quick! I have no time to tell you now.

We must get to the Rock Island depot. Have you your revolvers with you?"

"Yes," said Alexander, producing his trusty weapons and inspecting them carefully.

"Then come with me, for we have not a moment to spare."

With one strong pull the boat reached the shore. Our hero hastened up the bank, closely followed by Alexander, and ran toward the Rock Island depot.

Just as our hero and his companion dashed into the train shed a man with a slouch hat pulled down over his face ran for a train which was slowly moving out of the station.

That man was Rudolf Belmont!

Chapter 5

THWARTED

OUR hero, it will be recalled, saw Rudolf Belmont running to catch the train. He redoubled his speed.

As Rudolf Belmont swung on the last platform, Cyril followed closely.

He seized the object of his pursuit. They grappled and fell from the train.

Our hero fell underneath. "Curse you; though you had nine lives, like a cat, your time has come now," hissed Rudolf Belmont, drawing a revolver and pointing it at our hero's head.

At that instant a pistol shot rang out and Rudolf Belmont emitted a cry of pain.

The revolver fell from his hand.

The faithful Alexander had put a bullet through the villain's hand.

The next instant Cyril was on his feet and Rudolf Belmont was in the custody of a stalwart policeman.

"You came at an opportune moment," said our hero, with a quiet smile, as he shook hands with Alexander. Then, turning to the policeman, he said: "Your prisoner has in his possession certain papers which I wish to secure, after which you may take him to prison."

The policeman touched his cap respectfully and Cyril removed the bundle of papers from Rudolf Belmont's inner pocket.

Rudolf Belmont was led away, cursing.

Chapter 6

United

"MOTHER!"

"Cyril!"

It was indeed a happy evening at the magnificent home in Michigan Boulevard.

"I have brought you the papers, mother," said Cyril, modestly.

"My brave boy!" she murmured, with pardonable pride.

"We must not forget your friend, who so bravely came to your succor," and she handed Alexander a $1000 note.

Little remains to be told.

Rudolf Belmont served a life sentence in Joliet. Cyril Smith lives happily with his mother, Mrs. Fisher, who is as young and beautiful as ever. Often, on pleasant evenings, they entertain at dinner a thoughtful man with a brown mustache and genteel suit of dark material. That man is a member of the Knights of Pythias, but if we look again we will see that he is none other than our old friend, Alexander.

The End

The Glendon Mystery;

or,

Eddie Parks, the Newsboy Detective

"AHA!"
OUR HERO
SYBIL
SAVED!
McCUTCHEON

THE GLENDON MYSTERY; or, EDDIE PARKS, THE NEWSBOY DETECTIVE

Chapter 1

The Mystery

THE Chief of Police of the great city of Chicago sat alone in his office.

He wore a perturbed look. Ever and anon an ejaculation escaped his lips.

It had been a week since the Glendon robbery in the Lake Shore Drive, and the sleuths had not yet discovered a clew as to the identity of the robbers.

The thieves had entered the Glendon mansion at night, carried away $3000 in money, $60,000 worth of diamonds and an autographed letter of an English nobleman declining an invitation to dinner, valued at $8000.

Worst of all, they had abducted Sibyl Glendon, the beautiful and accomplished daughter of Hugh Glendon, the millionaire. Thus far every effort of the police to trace the thieves had been baffled.

Day by day the mystery deepened.

Little wonder that the Chief of Police was unhappy as he paced back and forth in the magnificent apartment.

Suddenly a servant entered the room, and, making a low bow, said:

"The Newsboy Detective wishes to see you."

The great official gave a sudden start.

"The very one!" he exclaimed.

The next instant he was clasping the hand of Eddie Parks!

Chapter 2

Two Men

LET us take a second look at our hero as he sits on the elegant divan chatting with the Chief of Police. He has an open countenance, a flashing eye and a determined look. Such is the youth who at the age of nine has made himself a most celebrated detective in the great city of Chicago, the terror of all criminals.

"And so you think you have a clew?" asked the Chief, with a keen glance at our hero.

"I am on the trail," replied our young sleuth, accepting the fragrant cigar tendered him. "I know the whereabouts of the maiden."

"This is indeed remarkable," said the Chief. "How did you come into possession of this information?"

In a few words our hero told of having seen two suspicious-looking men talking in a Jackson Street café. Disguising himself as a flower girl he had sauntered up to the table and had heard enough of their conversation to assure himself that they were implicated in the abduction of Sibyl Glendon. For three days he shadowed the two men all of the time. One lived on the north side. The other lived on the south side.

All of the facts were fitting together.

"Aha, this grows interesting!" exclaimed the Chief.

Our hero smiled modestly. He told how he followed the men into a restaurant. They went to a lavatory to wash their hands. He waited until they removed their cuffs and then he stole their cuffs and escaped.

"And why did you purloin the cuffs?" asked the Chief.

"I wished to be sure of their names!" exclaimed our hero. "They had been patronizing a Chinese laundry and the names were in Chinese. Fortunately, I have studied that language."

So saying, our hero handed the Chief a slip of paper bearing the names of Granville Armytage and Herbert Blusco.

The Chief stepped to his desk and wrote as follows:

All members of the Police Department are instructed to obey orders given by the bearer.
(Signed) CHIEF

"You may need some money," said he, and he pressed a $100 bill into our hero's hand.

Five minutes later a man with full white beard and snowy hair emerged from the city hall, and, boarding a west-bound car, rode rapidly away.

Few, indeed, would have recognized beneath this disguise the well-known figure of the Newsboy Detective!

Chapter 3

A Prisoner

"NEVER!"

These were the words spoken in a ringing tone by Sibyl Glendon. Herbert Blusco cringed before her gaze.

Sibyl Glendon was indeed a regal beauty, and she was never more beautiful than when she said the above words to Herbert Blusco.

A mass of golden hair fell about her shoulders and the black velvet dress which she wore served to intensify the pallor of her countenance.

The scene was in a palatial apartment rich with draperies and works of art.

Herbert Blusco hesitated for a moment, and then, with a muttered oath, he left the apartment, locking the door after him.

Sibyl Glendon threw herself on an upholstered couch and burst into a flood of tears.

Here, in the midst of this splendor, she was a prisoner!

Herbert Blusco had laid his plans well.

He had stolen the Glendon diamonds and the letter from the English nobleman in order to drive Sibyl's proud family from its honored place in society.

To crown his infamy he had abducted the beautiful society girl and was holding her captive until she would promise to become his bride.

All these thoughts passed through the brain of Sibyl Glendon as she reclined on the couch. A low moan escaped her lips.

Suddenly there was a sound of breaking glass and an arrow fell at Sibyl's feet. She picked it up. Wrapped around the arrow was a note. She read it with trembling hands.

These were the words:

Be brave. A friend is near.

"Thank heaven!" she exclaimed, and fainted.

Chapter 4

Help!

SIBYL GLENDON was aroused from her swoon by the sound of footfalls in the hallway.

She shrank back and listened with bated breath.

Herbert Blusco and his friend Granville Armytage entered the room. They wore full dress suits and were smoking cigarettes.

"Come here!" said Granville Armytage hoarsely.

At these words a withered old hag entered the room and leered at our heroine, who emitted a low cry of fear.

"This is the girl," said Granville Armytage; "keep a close watch on her. If she behaves, use her well. If not—" and he made a significant gesture.

Sibyl fell back on the couch and wept softly.

With a cruel laugh, Herbert Blusco and Granville Armytage strode from the room.

Scarcely had they departed when Sibyl heard a voice close to her ear: "Fear not. I am here to save you."

She looked up and saw the old woman standing by her side.

"What do you mean?" she asked, in doubt and fear.

"This!"

In a moment the disguise was thrown off and Sibyl was face to face with the Newsboy Detective..

"That face!" she shrieked, gazing at our hero.

With feverish haste she drew from her bosom a locket encrusted with jewels, which she gazed at.

"Brother!" she exclaimed. "To think that I have found you—and here!"

With an effort our hero repressed his emotions.

"Darling sister," said he, "we must escape from this place. You are in the clutches of two desperate villains, who will scruple at nothing."

At that instant the room filled with smoke and the clanging of bells was heard outside.

Our hero ran to the window, and his face blanched.

"Courage, sister!" he exclaimed. "The house is on fire!"

Chapter 5

The Holocaust

FIRE!"

"Fire!"

"Fire!"

The wild alarm rang throughout the great city of Chicago and countless thousands assembled to witness the conflagration.

The great stone mansion of the Blusco family was being devoured by the hungry flames. For blocks around the wildest excitement prevailed, and the scene beggared description.

Suddenly a moan of horror swept through a vast assemblage. There, in the topmost window, stood a youth, supporting in his arms a beautiful young lady.

At first the multitude was frozen with horror, and then a mighty cheer went up, for they had recognized in the youth at the window none other than our hero, the Newsboy Detective!

With lightning rapidity the firemen raised the tallest ladder. It was still thirty feet from the window!

The ledge on which our hero stood was enveloped in flames.

"Courage," he whispered.

Then he leaped.

Through the air he shot like a rocket. Sibyl clung to him desperately.

He caught the top round of the ladder with his left hand, and for a moment dangled in the air far above the horrified spectators.

Then he drew himself up and whispered to his fair burden.

"Saved!" she exclaimed, and fainted.

Chapter 6

Run to Earth

AFTER setting fire to the house, Herbert Blusco and Granville Armytage stepped into a carriage and were driven away to the grand ball to be given by Mrs. Clarence St. Clair.

"Are you sure they will perish in the flames?" asked Herbert Blusco, with an oath.

"Certainly," replied Granville Armytage, with an oath.

At that moment the carriage stopped before the brilliantly lighted St. Clair mansion.

Herbert Blusco and Granville Armytage were soon mingling with the merry throng. Few, to have seen them, would have suspected that they were desperate criminals.

At midnight the ball was at its height. Herbert Blusco was entering the ballroom with Mrs. Clarence St. Clair on his arm, when he felt a heavy hand on his shoulder and a voice said: "You are my prisoner."

With a gasp he turned.

There stood the Newsboy Detective!

At that moment a pistol shot rang out.

Granville Armytage had shot himself in the conservatory.

Chapter 7

Home Again

LITTLE remains to be told.

When Herbert Blusco was searched by the police, the Glendon diamonds and the letter from the English nobleman were found in his possession. Next day he was sentenced to prison for life.

Eddie Parks was offered a home with his sister, but he preferred to continue selling papers and ferreting out mysteries. The $10,000 reward paid him for recovering the diamonds he used in completing the Home for Newsboys.

The End

Eddie Parks to the Rescue;

or,

The National Bank Robbery

VAULT
MIDNIGHT!
McCUTCHEON

EDDIE PARKS TO THE RESCUE; or,
THE NATIONAL BANK ROBBERY

Chapter 1

The Plotters

"HOW much did you say?"

"One million four hundred and sixty-three thousand dollars."

"A good night's work."

"E'en so."

Three men seated in an elegant private apartment of a metropolitan hotel exchanged significant glances.

"Are you sure that you can hypnotize Hiram Clivington?" asked one.

"I am positive of it. I can put him under the hypnotic influence without waking him. Then he will tell us the combination to the vault; after that all is plain sailing."

"Blinky" Briggs, Eau Claire George and

F. Morton Bunker, three of the most skillful and desperate burglars ever known in the annals of crime, chuckled hoarsely.

At that moment a voice was heard in the hallway. It was the voice of a woman singing "On the Banks of the Wabash." The door opened and a chambermaid of prepossessing appearance entered the room.

"Did you ring for towels, gents?" asked she in a pleasant manner.

"No," replied Eau Claire George.

Without another word the chambermaid began tidying up the room, while the three men continued to converse in low tones. Presently they arose and left the room.

A peculiar expression was visible on the face of the chambermaid.

"We shall see," she remarked.

Chapter 2

Hypnotized

MIDNIGHT!

Hiram Clivington, cashier of the Eleventh National Bank, lay asleep in his sumptuous apartment. All the bedclothes were of silk and satin, and it could be seen that he had jeweled buttons on his pajamas.

All was silent save for the measured breathing of the handsome gray-bearded man in the magnificent bed.

Suddenly the door opened noiselessly and three masked men glided into the room. One of them advanced on tiptoe to the bed-side and made mystic signs and passes above the recumbent form.

"It is well," he whispered.

Then, taking Hiram Clivington's hand in his, he said: "Tell me the combination to the main vault."

Without opening his eyes, the cashier slowly said:

"Fifteen—two, fifteen—four, to the right, to the left, three sixes, then turn around and go the other way."

"Have you got it down?" asked Eau Claire George, the hypnotist.

"Yes," answered his companion F. Mor-ton Bunker.

Without another word the three men hurried from the room!

Chapter 3

A Night Ride

THE three men escaped from the house and walked several blocks, finally stopping at a dark corner, where they waited for ten minutes or more.

Then a carriage came rolling along the street and stopped at the corner. On the box sat a muffled figure.

"You understand?" asked "Blinky" Briggs of the driver.

"I understand," replied the driver, in a gruff voice.

"Then hurry," and the three men jumped into the conveyance.

The horses sprang away at a lively speed. The carriage rolled from side to side.

In a few minutes Eau Claire George looked out of the window and gave an exclamation of dismay.

"We are going in the wrong direction!" he shouted.

"Look!" ejaculated F. Morton Bunker, pointing out at the same moment through the glass front of the speeding carriage.

The driver had disappeared!

"Perdition!" was all Eau Claire George could say as he threw himself against the door. It would not yield.

The horses were running away, and the three men were locked in the carriage!

Chapter 4

Thwarted!

"Blinky" Briggs, Eau Claire George and F. Morton Bunker clung to their seats, expecting every moment that the carriage would be overturned.

At last the horses stopped from sheer exhaustion and the three desperadoes broke the glass from a window and crawled out.

They found themselves in West Pullman.

"Curse the carelessness of that driver!" said Eau Claire George. "We have lost valuable time."

"Blinky" Briggs mounted the driver's box and his two companions crawled back into the carriage again and were driven quickly toward the Eleventh National Bank.

It was 3 o'clock in the morning when they reached the bank building. Going to the alley back of the building, they crawled through a window and soon were at the vault door.

F. Morton Bunker read the combination and Eau Claire George turned the metallic tumblers. In a few minutes the great doors swung open.

"Aha!" said "Blinky" Briggs, as he stepped into the vault; but a moment later he gave a cry of rage.

The vault was empty!

Chapter 5

The Mystery

NEXT morning there was tremendous excitement in Chicago.

The Eleventh National Bank had been robbed of one million four hundred and sixty-three thousand dollars!

This vast sum had been taken from the vault, and yet the officials of the bank could not discover that the lock had been tampered with.

It was agreed that the money must have been taken by some one who knew the combination, and suspicion naturally fell on Hiram Clivington, he being the only one who was in on the secret.

The venerable and trusted cashier gave a strict account of his doings on the night of the robbery, but the directors of the bank were skeptical and relieved him of his place.

On the morning following the discovery of the robbery Hiram Clivington opened the vault and explained the combination to his successor J. H. Grief.

What was his surprise upon glancing into the vault to see there the one million four hundred and sixty-three thousand dollars!

Chapter 6

The Conspirators

THE fact that the stolen money had been returned to the bank caused great amazement, and seemed to prove beyond all doubt that Hiram Clivington was the guilty man. It was supposed that he had put the money back into the vault to save himself from prosecution. He protested his innocence, but to no avail.

J. H. Grief was made cashier, and the combination was changed.

In the meantime "Blinky" Briggs, Eau Claire George and F. Morton Bunker had been biding their time, baffled for the nonce, but still determined to obtain possession of that one million four hundred and sixty-three thousand dollars, if possible.

They determined to visit the home of J. H. Grief by night, obtain the new combination by hypnotic influence and get into the vault.

Bold and determined men, these.

Chapter 7

A Surprise

MIDNIGHT again!

The three desperadoes crept into the bedchamber of J. H. Grief. On the snowy couch lay a stalwart man with a full growth of red beard. Eau Claire George stood above the sleeping man, moved his hands to and fro. Suddenly a violent tremor seized him.

"I have met a will that is stronger than mine!" he gasped.

At that moment a revolver was pointed straight at his face, and the man on the bed said:

"Don't move or I'll shoot!"

Before "Blinky" Briggs or F. Morton Bunker could spring to his asssistance, they were pinioned from behind by two burly policemen.

"What does this mean?" demanded Eau Claire George.

"It means that you have been trapped," responded the man on the bed, as he removed the red beard.

Eau Claire George gave a shriek of mortal terror.

Before him he saw Eddie Parks, the Newsboy Detective!!

Chapter 8

Retribution

"YOU are, indeed, a remarkable youth," said the president of the bank, shaking our hero by the hand.

"One would hardly expect a boy of ten to capture three such desperate characters. Pray narrate to me how you accomplished your purpose."

Our hero blushed modestly as he told his story.

"When I learned that these three miscreants were here in Chicago, I knew it was for no good purpose," said he. "Accordingly I went to the hotel at which they were temporarily domiciled, and, disguising myself as a chambermaid, gained admittance to their room and overheard their foul conspiracy to hypnotize Mr. Clivington and obtain the combination to the vault. Accordingly I preceded them to Mr. Clivington's house and secreted myself under his bed. When they obtained the combination from him I took it down very carefully. As soon as they had left I descended from the second story by a water pipe and hurried away to where their carriage was in waiting. It was the work of a few minutes to overpower the driver and put on his clothes. I broke the inside door handles so that the doors could not be opened except from the outside. Then I drove up to where the villains were waiting. My disguise was perfect. They got into the carriage. I started the horses south instead of north, lashed them into a run and leaped from the box. I knew the men could not escape until the horses stopped, so I had time to go to the bank, open the vault by means of the combination I had obtained under the bed and remove the one million four hundred and sixty-three thousand dollars to a place of safety. Two hours later the robbers came and opened the vault, only to find it empty. Next night, feeling sure that they would not renew the attempt at once, I replaced the money in the vault. Knowing these men as I do, I was satisfied that they would try to practice their infernal devices on Mr. Grief. Accordingly I sent him a bogus telegram calling him out of town, and went to his room disguised as him and accompanied by two trusty officers of the law. The rest you know."

"You are indeed a bright boy, and have a great future before you," said the bank president.

Little remains to be told.

Mr. Clivington was restored to his position as cashier and the three robbers were given long terms in the penitentiary. Eddie Parks was offered a reward of $25,000 by the bank. At first he refused it, but afterwards he accepted it and devoted it to useful charities.

THE END

Clarence Allen, the Hypnotic Boy Journalist;

or,

The Mysterious Disappearance of the United States Government Bonds

EXPENSE ACCOUNT
J. WINDSOR FROST
CITY EDITOR
ARTISTS
BLOOD
THE GREAT EDITOR
OUR HERO
BAFFLED!
McCUTCHEON

CLARENCE ALLEN, THE HYPNOTIC BOY JOURNALIST; or, THE MYSTERIOUS DISAPPEARANCE OF THE UNITED STATES GOVERNMENT BONDS

Chapter 1

To Work

IT was in the office of the *Chicago Daily Beacon!* J. Windsor Frost, the editor, sat in his palatial apartment, where the light fell softly through the stained-glass windows and the walls were tastefully decorated with articles of bric-a-brac and vertu.

J. Windsor Frost was a handsome man and a neat diamond flashed in his shirt front.

Suddenly he aroused himself and an expectant smile came to his face.

A manly youth of twelve years of age entered the room and stood facing the great editor. He had a strikingly handsome face and an eagle eye. On his breast glittered a star, indicating that he was a representative of the press. A notebook and a well-sharpened lead pencil protruded from his breast pocket.

This is our first view of Clarence Allen, the hypnotic boy journalist.

"Ah, you have come," said the great editor.

"Yes, Mr. Frost, I am always ready to answer the call of duty," said our hero, modestly.

Without further ado the great editor handed the following clipping to the boy journalist:

GREAT EXCITEMENT

Our city was thrown into a fever of excitement last evening by the announcement that Erastus Hare, one of our oldest and most respected citizens, had been robbed of $37,000 worth of United States government bonds by some unknown miscreant. The culprit entered Mr. Hare's bedroom through a window and attacked our old friend and subscriber with a knife. Afterwards he took the bonds and escaped. As we go to press he has not been caught. Little knots of men may be seen standing on the corners discussing the topic in low tones. Great excitement prevails.

"The item you have just read was printed in this morning's *Beacon*," said J. Windsor Frost. "This is the greatest criminal case that ever came under my observation. Can you find the thief?"

"I can," replied Clarence, and, drawing his notebook, he hastily made a few notes.

At that moment he heard a suspicious noise outside the window. He ran to see what could have been the cause.

A masked man was rapidly descending to the ground by means of a rope.

They had been overheard!

Chapter 2

The Footprint

AFTER providing himself with a dark lantern and other needful articles, Clarence Allen, the hypnotic boy journalist, summoned a carriage and was driven rapidly to the Hare mansion.

Here all was confusion.

Our hero took immediate charge of the premises and made a minute examination of the room in which the assault had taken place. He measured the bedstead, counted the pictures and cut a small strip out of the carpet. Afterward he went outside and examined the ground. Suddenly he saw a deep footprint in the soft earth.

"Aha!" said he.

Taking the necessary articles from his pocket, he made a plaster cast of the footprints.

"I have a clew," said he, and, drawing his notebook, he made a few notes.

At that moment a bullet whistled by!

Chapter 3

Desperate

WITH Clarence Allen to think was to act.

When the deadly bullet sped by his head

he knew that the thieves had recognized him as a representative of the press, probably because of the star on his coat.

Without further ado he rushed to a telephone and called up the office of the *Daily Beacon* and expressed a wish to converse with J. Windsor Frost, the great editor.

"Hello!"

"Hello!"

"Who is this?"

"This is J. Windsor Frost, the editor. And you?"

"I am Clarence Allen, the hypnotic boy journalist. I desire—"

But J. Windsor Frost heard no more.

The wire had been cut!

Chapter 4

Quick Work

WHAT was our hero to do?

For a moment only he hesitated. Then he rushed to the window.

It was thirty feet to the ground below.

A trolley car was approaching.

"I have no time to spare," he exclaimed, and jumped to the pavement.

Leaping to the trolley car he pushed the motorman aside, and, seizing the crank, sent the car flying along the street at a speed of twenty-five miles an hour.

The conductor of the car attempted to pull him away. With a well-directed blow our hero sent him flying.

Women passengers shrieked in terror and the street was in a panic.

Little cared Clarence Allen, the hypnotic boy journalist.

Suddenly applying the brake in front of the office of the *Daily Beacon*, he ran wildly into the office of J. Windsor Frost and showed him what he had written in his note-book.

"Great Heavens!" exclaimed the great editor. "And now what do you propose doing?"

Clarence's eyes flashed as he replied:

"I am going to put the bloodhounds on the trail!"

Clarence Allen, Boy Journalist

Chapter 5

The Stone House

THE *Daily Beacon*, like all other great newspapers, had a pack of genuine Siberian bloodhounds, for tracking criminals.

Our hero, after making out an expense account, selected two of the largest and fiercest bloodhounds and showed them the plaster cast of the footprint which he had taken at the Hare residence.

The intelligent animals knew at a glance what was expected of them, and in a few moments they were on the scent, followed by our alert young hero, Clarence Allen, the hypnotic boy journalist, who carried a revolver tightly clenched in his right hand.

For nearly an hour no one spoke.

Then the dogs stopped in front of an old stone house.

"This is the place," said Clarence Allen, concealing himself to await developments.

After a moment he chanced to look around, and his blood froze in his veins.

Some one had stolen the dogs!

Chapter 6

Hypnotized

IT will be remembered that we left our hero concealed in the thicket.

He remained here for some time, and then, making sure that he had eluded his pursuers, he ventured forth and made a hasty examination of the old stone house.

It was a dark night and the wind rustled through the elm trees.

Only one window was lighted, and it was on the second floor.

"They are there," said our hero, and, procuring a coil of rope with a hook in the end of it, he made a fastening to the ledge of the second-story window and climbed up until he could peer in at the window.

Three bearded men sat at a table talking in hoarse tones. Our hero felt a thrill when he heard his own name mentioned.

"It is understood, then," said the leader, "that we meet an hour from now at the blasted oak to divide the money."

" 'Tis well," said the other two.

"And then we will leave this country forever."

"Hold," cried a stentorian voice, and with a crashing of glass, Clarence Allen, the hypnotic boy journalist, leaped through the window and confronted them.

For a moment they were surprised, and then with fearful oaths they drew their weapons.

"Your time has come," snarled the leader of the gang.

Three revolvers were pointed straight at our intrepid young hero!

Could aught save him?

Clarence Allen did not flinch.

Gazing steadily at the leader of the band, he lifted his hands and moved them gently through the air.

The ruffian fell backward to the floor and the weapon dropped from his palsied hand.

Our hero turned quickly to the two other villains, who stood in mute surprise.

It was the work of a moment to put them under the hypnotic influence and take away their weapons.

"At last!" he said, and, taking out his book, he made full notes of the proceedings.

Chapter 7

Justice

HAVING hypnotized the villains, it was an easy task for our hero to learn from the leader of the band the hiding place of the stolen bonds. They were found under a loose tiling in the fireplace and returned to their owner, who speedily recovered from his injuries.

Little remains to be told.

The *Daily Beacon* printed a half-column account, under glaring headlines, of the capture of the desperadoes by the hypnotic boy journalist.

As for the thieves, they were promptly sent to prison on the testimony of our hero, who achieved a great reputation for his courageous conduct and was soon after admitted to membership in the League of American Wheelmen, a distinction which few merit and a glory which few achieve.

THE END

The Steel Box;

or,

The Robbers of Rattlesnake Gulch

FOILED!
"CURSE THE LUCK!"
C McCutcheon

THE STEEL BOX; or,
THE ROBBERS OF RATTLESNAKE GULCH

Chapter 1

The Cipher Message

"A COMMUNICATION for you, sir."
With these words a youthful messenger placed an envelope on the desk of the mighty railroad official, Rodney Russell, president of the Lake Michigan & Iowa Southern Railway. The great man turned in his revolving chair, which must have cost a large sum of money, and picked up the envelope.

Rodney Russell was a stalwart and handsome man with a long and flowing brown mustache. His pleated shirt front bore two superb diamonds, and he had other marks of being a real gentleman.

"I cannot understand this," he said, half aloud, when he had finished reading the epistle.

"Is it written in English?" asked the messenger, who stood near at hand.

"Out of the room!" commanded the president, sternly.

The youth retired and the mighty official once more scrutinized the strange communication.

Suddenly the door opened and a handsome man in light clothes, spring overcoat, blond side whiskers and a neat rattan cane stepped into the room.

"You received a letter," he said.

"I did."

"Do you understand it?"

"I do not."

"Will you permit me to look at it?"

"Whom are you?" he asked, for he had attended business college.

"A friend. I may be able to do you a service."

The president gave him the epistle.

As the stranger glanced at it he blanched perceptibly.

"Aha! Just as I thought!" he exclaimed. "It is the cipher!"

What he read was as follows:

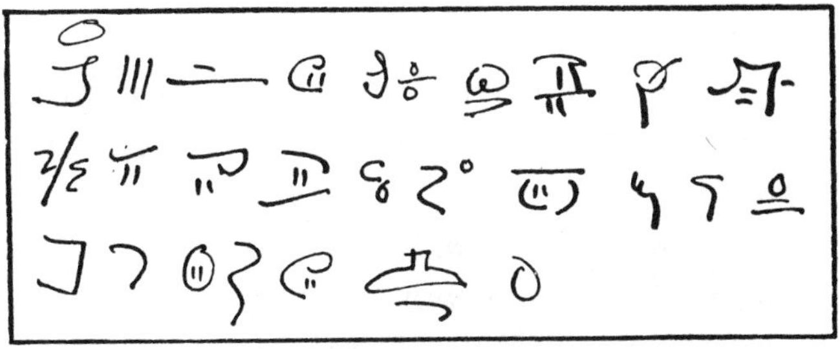

"Do you know what this means?" asked the stranger with a grim smile.

"No."

"It means that the Sunrise Express is to be held up in Rattlesnake Gulch to-night!"

"Heavens!"

With a low moan the president sank to the floor in a swoon. The stranger rushed from the room.

At that moment two pistol shots rang out on the frosty air!

Chapter 2

The Pursuit

IT was two o'clock.

In the roundhouse of the Lake Michigan & Iowa Southern Railway a dozen huge locomotives, panting under a full head of steam, waited for orders.

The attendants were at work around the monsters, rubbing the metallic parts and testing them.

Suddenly a bearded man rushed through the doorway. He wore a sweater, but no coat or vest. His eyes blazed with excitement.

"I want a fireman!" he shouted.

"I am a fireman," replied a muscular young man, stepping forward.

"Then get on this engine. We must be off."

"Have you the orders?"

"Never mind the orders," said the bearded stranger, drawing a revolver. "Get on that engine."

The fireman obeyed with alacrity.

The stranger followed.

With a fearful puffing and the grinding of wheels, the immense Mogul Number Eleven moved out of the roundhouse and gathered speed as it rolled through the yards.

"The Sunrise Express has four hours' start," said the stranger, who stood at the throttle, "but I will overtake her."

The great engine increased its speed and soon houses, fields, telegraph poles and villages went reeling by in lightning procession.

"I might have wired the express to wait for me, but I do not wish anyone to suspect," he said.

The fireman shoveled incessantly.

The whole landscape flashed by in one whirling and confused blur.

The man at the throttle looked at his watch.

"Good!" he ejaculated.

For the train was making 147 miles an hour!

Chapter 3

THE EXPLOSION!

IT was dusk.

The Sunrise Express was flying, like a streaming comet, across the flat plains that lie to the west of Copperas Junction.

The rear brakeman had just throttled a passenger for asking a question, and was now standing on the back platform trying to get some more coal dust on his neck.

He saw a speck of light far back along the tracks. It became larger and brighter. The Express was being pursued!

He rushed to the conductor, who signaled to the engineer:

"More speed!"

They went to the back platform. The headlight came nearer and nearer.

"Curse the luck!" shouted the conductor. "What does it mean?"

The Express was making seventy-five miles an hour, but the engine gained and gained, until the headlight threw a bright glare over the rear platform where the terror-stricken conductor and brakeman were clinging.

As these two looked they saw a figure crawl out of the cab of the locomotive behind, clamber along the top and then climb the smokestack.

He balanced for a moment on top of the smokestack and then leaped forward and caught with one hand the railing on the platform of the car ahead.

Just as he drew himself up there was a terrific explosion!

The boiler of the pursuing locomotive had blown up!

The Sunrise Express plunged forward into the darkness!

Chapter 4

The Robbery

MIDNIGHT!

In one of the deep recesses of Rattlesnake Gulch three men waited. They were none other than the leaders of the famous

Dalton gang. All three were heavily armed and wore masks.

They spoke in hoarse whispers, such being the habit of all practiced robbers.

"Are you sure the money is on this train?" asked one.

"Yes," replied the leader, who was none other than Bill Dalton. "There's a cool million in the box in the express car. It's in currency and gold. Now, then, if the train don't stop to take water, pull the switch. Do you understand?"

"We do," replied the others, huskily.

"Get ready, then."

Even as he spoke there was a distant whistle and in a few moments the rumbling of the train.

Fortune seemed to favor the robbers.

The train came to a stop at the water tank. One desperado jumped into the cab of the locomotive and covered the engineer and fireman. The other two went to the express car and commanded that the door be opened.

"Open the car or we'll blow it up with dynamite," shouted Bill Dalton.

The door opened and the frightened express messenger asked in a trembling voice, "What do you want?"

"We want the steel box, right away," was the gruff reply of the ringleader.

The messenger dragged the heavy box to the door and said: "Take it, but please spare my life."

The two robbers laughed scornfully. Bill Dalton shouted to his comrade in the cab, who told the engineer to pull out at full speed, on pain of death.

The engineer obeyed.

The train rolled away, leaving the three robbers in possession of their plunder.

"The slickest job I ever did," said Bill Dalton, gleefully.

The three robbers lifted the steel box and hurried away into the darkness.

Just as the first gray of the dawn was showing in the east, Bill Dalton and his two villainous companions were seated in a rough cabin somewhat sheltered by a straggling growth of cottonwood trees.

Bill Dalton knelt before the big steel box and was directing powerful blows against the lock with a cold chisel and hammer.

"Hurry up!" shouted one of his companions. "We must divide the swag and be miles away from here before noon."

Bill Dalton struck another blow, and the shattered lock fell to the floor.

"There!" he exclaimed, and lifted the lid.

Even as he did so he gave a gasp of terror.

His two companions sat chilled with fear.

A youth of intrepid appearance was sitting up in the box, covering the bandits with two glittering revolvers!

"Don't make a move, or I will shoot," he said calmly.

He gave a short whistle, and six armed men came hurriedly through the door and seized the robbers.

"Tricked!" shrieked Bill Dalton, and looking at the youth with baleful hatred he hissed between his teeth: "Curse you! Who are you?"

"I," said the youth in the box, "am Eddie Parks, the Newsboy Detective!"

The Steel Box

Chapter 5

Back in Chicago

SEATED in a private room at a fashionable Chicago club, Eddie Parks told President Rodney Russell of the Lake Michigan & Iowa Southern Railway of the manner in which he had captured the famous outlaws.

"Seeing a man of suspicious appearance enter your office, I decided to find out the object of his visit," said our hero, with a modest smile.

"Accordingly I disguised myself and called on you. As soon as I saw the cipher message I knew what it meant. It was evidently sent by some member of the gang who had a grudge against Bill Dalton, and who was afraid to send a letter in his own handwriting."

"Ah, I see," said the great railroad official.

"As soon as I realized the danger I changed my disguise and hurried to the roundhouse, where I took forcible possession of a locomotive and pursued the Express.

As soon as I leaped to the express train I told the conductor of the impending danger, and he promised to assist me in any plan looking toward the meting out of justice to the miscreants. Knowing of the Daltons' cabin retreat, I organized a posse from among the passengers and sent them to the cabin to remain in hiding until I whistled. The rest you know—of how I secreted myself in the box and waited until the opportune moment arrived."

"To think that a boy of ten should succeed after all the great detective agencies had failed!" said the great man, musingly. "You are a clever youth."

"I did my duty," said our hero, with downcast eyes.

Little remains to be told.

The Daltons were either hanged or sent to prison again. Eddie Parks refused the $50,000 offered by the railway company and express company, saying that he preferred to go back among his loved companions and sell newspapers.

THE END

Rollo Johnson, the Boy Inventor;

or,

The Demon Bicycle and Its Daring Rider

AMPERES
PLANS
OHMS
VOLTS
PLANS
OUR HERO AT WORK
CHIEF JUSTICE WAITE
McCUTCHEON
VICTORY!!
BANG!
BANG!
BANG!

ROLLO JOHNSON, THE BOY INVENTOR; or, THE DEMON BICYCLE AND ITS DARING RIDER

Chapter 1

The Secret

"AT LAST!"

Rollo Johnson arose from his work as he gave vent to the above.

His friend, Paul Jefferson, who stood by his side, asked: "Are you sure you have succeeded?"

"Yes," replied Rollo, a proud flush coming to his cheek. "With this bicycle I am quite sure I can make the fastest time that has ever been made."

Well might our hero flush, for now at the age of eight he had accomplished what Edison had failed to do. He had built a bicycle to be operated by electricity!

Standing in his workshop with Paul Jefferson by his side, he explained in a few words the secret of his invention.

He had filled the tubing with compacted batteries and had joined them together by copper wires, thus utilizing the vacuum. At the point in the ball-bearing axle where the currents convexed, a flexolever had been placed, with the ohms operating directly on the hub. By this contrivance our hero was enabled to use a gearing of 282, as easily as another rider would use 68 or 72.

"It is indeed wonderful," said Paul Jefferson. "After four years of incessant toil you are to be rewarded."

"Yes," replied Rollo, musingly. "Tomorrow I shall win the mile championship on my wheel and then I will be famous."

A grating laugh startled them.

They turned and beheld Hector Legrand, the millionaire capitalist.

A cold, cruel smile flitted across his face.

"Rollo Johnson, I heard the statement you just made," said he, insultingly. "If you dare put this invention of yours on the market you will ruin me and mine, and I will kill you."

Our hero laughed defiantly. With a muttered curse Hector Legrand drew a dagger and sprang at our hero.

As he did so, Rollo stepped quickly backward and touched an electric button connected with galvanic plates under the floor.

With a maniacal shriek Hector Legrand fell to the floor and lay there quivering.

Chapter 2

The Race!

ROLLO JOHNSON well knew that his enemies were desperate and accordingly he had taken every precaution.

He had imparted the electric shock to Hector Legrand at the critical moment, for the millionaire's dagger was about to be imbedded in our hero's breast.

When Hector Legrand recovered from the shock he left the place, much crestfallen.

Rollo bade Paul Jefferson an affectionate good night, and soon after retired, for he wished to be well rested in anticipation of the great race for the championship of America.

Next morning he arose bright and early and proceeded to the race track, where thousands had already assembled.

It was known that our hero was the inventor of the demon bicycle, and there was a buzz of wonder and admiration as Rollo came upon the track, attired in a neat costume of red, white and blue. To all appearances his wheel was the same as those used by the other riders.

Hooper, the favorite in the race, approached our hero and said, tauntingly, "You are a mere stripling, and it is presumptuous of you to enter the championship race."

"I will bide my time," said Rollo, for he was a gentleman at heart.

A moment later the riders in the championship race were called to the tape and the word "go" was given.

Eight wheels flashed away in the sunlight.

Hooper was leading, Gardiner was second and Smikels was third. Our hero was last of all, pursuing an even pace, a smile lighting up his pale and handsome face.

At the quarter mile he was ten lengths behind.

At the half mile he seemed hopelessly beaten.

Suddenly there was a shout.

Rollo had touched the button and released the powerful current.

His wheel shot forward like a flash of lightning.

He passed the other riders in a twinkling.

The amphitheater rang with wild cheers. He had won by twenty lengths!

The last half mile had been made in 14 seconds!

Chapter 3

The Plans

WITH a light heart Rollo returned home, having won the championship of America.

As he entered the house a sad sight presented itself. His father and mother and his elder brother Claude were seated in the parlor weeping bitterly.

"Why so sad on this day when all should be joy?" asked our hero.

"Alas!" replied his mother, kissing him affectionately, "some one has stolen the plans."

"Stolen the plans!" he gasped.

"Yes, Rollo; the only copy in existence was left lying on the table in your workshop, and some miscreant has purloined it."

"If I do not recover those plans my four years of investigation will have been in vain," said Rollo, thoughtfully. "I will follow the thieves to the world's end!" and leaping on his demon bicycle, he rode away like the wind!

Chapter 4

The River

IT was dusk.

In a dingy basement near the murky Chicago River Hector Legrand sat at a table with four swarthy men, heavily armed.

Before them on the table were the plans for Rollo Johnson's demon bicycle. They were conversing in hoarse tones.

"I have the plans," said Hector Legrand, "but my revenge is not yet complete. The boy must be put out of the way."

His four companions growled fiercely.

At that instant a volt of lightning shot across the room. There was a blinding flash and the five men fell from their chairs stunned by the shock.

Rollo Johnson had crept down the stairway and turned upon them the full force of his portable automo-battery.

As the villains struggled to their feet they saw our hero disappearing up the stairway. He had captured the plans.

With shrieks and curses they drew their weapons and pursued him.

Rollo mounted his wheel and dashed southward.

A dozen bullets whizzed by him.

He looked ahead.

The street along which he was flying led to the open river!

There was no escape to right or left!
Behind him were the murderous pursuers!
Ahead of him yawned the dark stream!
What was he to do?

Chapter 5

The Escape

HECTOR LEGRAND and his villainous associates emitted yells of triumph when they saw our hero riding madly toward the open river.

Rollo heard their demoniacal cries and he knew that capture meant certain death.

Pressing the electric button on his wheel he flew forward at a terrific speed.

At the river's brink he lifted his front wheel.

The bicycle shot into the air with the swiftness of an arrow.

Bang! Bang! Bang! went the revolvers.

Then there were howls of rage.

Rollo had landed safely on the other side!

Chapter 6

Retribution

AFTER his escape from the would-be assassins, Rollo's first act was to notify the police of Hector Legrand's attempt to steal the plans.

The police went to Hector Legrand's mansion to arrest him, but he had escaped, and was never again seen in Chicago.

His four associates were soon after arrested on another charge and sent to prison for life. Such is the fate of evildoers.

As for Rollo Johnson, he took his plans home and had his mother put them in a safe place.

Little remains to be told.

Our hero received a million dollars for his invention and achieved just fame, but he did not relinquish his study, and every day he may be seen in his workshop inventing some useful article for the betterment of mankind.

The End

The Boy Champion;

or,

America's Fair Name Defended

VICTORY!

THE BOY CHAMPION; or, AMERICA'S FAIR NAME DEFENDED

Chapter 1

The Defiance

"NO!"

George Webster's voice rang out clear and strong.

Mortimer Blake flushed and said:

"Have a care."

George Webster drew himself up proudly as he said:

"Mortimer Blake, I have told you that I would not engage in this pugilistic encounter were it not for the fact that I desire to provide for my dear mother and my sister Irene and protect the glorious Stars and Stripes."

As he spoke these words, his eyes filled with tears.

"Then you refuse?" asked Mortimer Blake, with a hiss.

"I am an American, and no American ever took a bribe," replied George, with flashing eye. "What do I care for one hundred thousand dollars, when my honor and my country's fair name are at stake?"

Once more his eyes filled with tears.

With a fearful oath Mortimer Blake drew a revolver.

Bang!

Bang!

He fired two shots straight at the heart of George Webster.

Chapter 2

Dark Work

"THE girl shall yet be mine!"

Such were the words spoken by Vincent Edgerton, and his eye had a baleful gleam. His remarks were addressed to the Water Rat, a bearded ruffian whose hideous features were an index to his depraved soul.

The two whispered together.

"To-night?"

"To-night."

"Alone?"

"Alone."

"Good."

Vincent Edgerton gazed keenly at his companion.

"Get poison into the boy's food!" he exclaimed. "He must not win this fight. If he loses, the family will be ruined and I can claim Irene for my own. Do you understand?"

"Yes," said the other, hoarsely.

They were going to poison George Webster!

Chapter 3

The Explosion

"IT is a fortunate circumstance that I had on my bullet-proof jacket," said George Webster to his trainer; "otherwise I would have been injured."

Bang! Bang!

Reddy Muldoon, the trainer, gazed at the young pugilist in admiration. "They will attempt anything to encompass our defeat," said he, "but we will thwart them."

The reader has no doubt recognized ere this the Chicago boy champion, George Webster, who at the age of thirteen had made for himself a reputation on both sides of the Atlantic and had vanquished a score of valiant fighters.

As he stood in the gymnasium chatting pleasantly with his trainer, his lithe frame could be seen to the best advantage. The great ridges of muscle stood out from his body and gave indication of his terrific strength.

"You appear pensive," said the faithful trainer, after a pause.

"Yes; I am thinking of Irene," replied our hero. "If I do not defeat the English champion to-morrow night I will lose the fifty thousand and my poor mother and darling sister will be reduced to a condition of comparative indigence. Our enemies are at work. The British government has its emissaries in our midst, and they will employ every means to accomplish their devilish purpose."

"Let us not fear," said Reddy. "The American people are with us."

"Yes," said our young hero, a teardrop glistening in his eye, "and I will defend the glorious star-spangled banner with my life."

At that instant there was a terrific explosion. The floor was shattered into a million fragments and the walls toppled and fell in. The ceiling rocked with a fearful crash.

Just as the ceiling fell our hero leaped from the doorway dragging his faithful trainer behind him.

Once outside, he breathed more freely and with a calm smile said:

"They have blown up the building with dynamite. We must be on the alert."

"Three cheers for the boy champion!" shouted an elderly man in the crowd that had assembled.

They were given with a will.

At that moment a note was handed our hero. He glanced at the contents and grew perceptibly pale.

Irene was missing!

Chapter 4

The Conspiracy

MORTIMER BLAKE, after firing two futile shots at George Webster's bullet-proof jacket, returned to the palatial hotel at which he was a guest. Stepping into the elevator he quickly ascended to the fourth floor and was ushered into a magnificent apartment, where two fashionably attired men sat at a marble table drinking champagne. One of these men was Lord Romney. The other was a secret agent of the British government, Guy Beresford.

"Curse the luck, I have failed!" exclaimed Mortimer Blake, sinking heavily to an ottoman.

"Did you blow up the building?" asked Lord Romney.

"Yes."

"And he escaped?"

"He did."

With a smothered curse Lord Romney arose and paced back and forth on the rich Brussels carpet.

"Should this American youth win, the British government will be disgraced before the world," he exclaimed. "I have received a message from the Prime Minister that he must be put out of the way at all hazards."

His companions exchanged significant looks.

"You mean—" began Guy Beresford.

"I mean that he must be drugged and carried away this very night."

"Cowards!"

The three conspirators turned hastily and then gave vent to ejaculations of surprise.

A beautiful young girl in pure white, with heavy chestnut curls falling about her shoulders, had stepped from behind the portière and stood with blazing eyes. In each hand she held a gleaming pistol.

"I have heard your nefarious plotting," said she, while her lip curled with scorn, "but your dastardly schemes will never succeed. George Webster is an American, and the American people will support him in his endeavor to protect the glorious Stars and Stripes, even as their forefathers protected our proud flag at Bunker Hill."

At these words the Englishmen winced.

"Stand back!" she exclaimed, as Lord Romney made a movement toward her. "Remember, I am protected by the flag!" saying which she drew the glorious emblem from her pocket and swept from the room.

Who was she?

She was Irene!

Chapter 5

To the Rescue

GEORGE WEBSTER had concluded his exercise for the day and sat with his trainer, Reddy Muldoon, reading the columns and columns which were printed in the newspapers.

"To think that in a few hours I am to meet Tug Smith, the greatest fighter that ever came from England," said our hero, musingly. "I feel that I must win that contest, for I realize, oh, so keenly, that the reputation of the United States of America is at stake."

Bang! Bang!

Two pistol shots suddenly rang out!

In ran a beautiful maiden.

It was Irene!

"What is it, darling sister?" asked our hero, folding Irene to his breast.

"I have just shot two men," she replied, smiling at him. "They were attempting to put this into your food."

She handed him a small vial. He looked at it and read:

"This is the work of the British Government!" exclaimed George Webster.

Chapter 6

VICTORY

"TIME!"

As the word was spoken, George Webster leaped nimbly to the center of the ring and faced his burly antagonist boldly.

A murmur of admiration ran through the vast crowd.

Although our hero was fully eighty pounds lighter than Tug Smith, his well-knit frame and catlike agility showed at a glance that he was no mean opponent.

Around his waist were the Stars and Stripes, the glorious emblem of the land of his birth.

On his face was a look of grim determination.

The interest was intense.

Tug Smith, a savage leer on his face, rushed at our hero and aimed a terrific blow. George Webster avoided it with the greatest ease.

"Bravo!" shouted the multitude.

Five times did the giant rush madly at our hero, and as many times did George Webster dodge the death-dealing blows.

Tug Smith paused to recover himself and our hero availed himself of the opportunity.

With a leap into the air, he struck the British champion a mighty blow on the jaw.

Tug Smith fell and lay helpless in the

ring while the boy champion bowed modestly in recognition of the thunderous applause.

He had won!

In response to the calls he made a brief and appropriate speech.

"I am proud [cheers] of my victory," said he, "because [cheers] the championship remains in America [cheers], under the glorious folds of the dear old Stars and Stripes."

At that moment there was a commotion in the crowd and four men were seen to pass from the building carrying the body of a man.

It was Lord Romney!

He had died of a broken heart!

Chapter 7

Mother and Sister

LITTLE remains to be told.

George Webster, clad in a rich dressing gown, sat in his beautiful home with his dear mother on one side of him and his darling sister Irene on the other side of him. He had been reading telegrams of congratulations from President McKinley, Chauncey M. Depew, Henry Watterson and other great Americans who rejoiced with him over the signal victory for the land of the free and the home of the brave.

"The police have captured Vincent Edgerton," said he to Irene. "He will trouble us no more."

A slight shudder passed through the girl's frame.

"Promise me that you will never again engage in a pugilistic contest," said our hero's mother, stroking his hair.

"I promise, mother," replied our hero, tenderly. "I promise that I will not do so, except in defense of the dear old Stars and Stripes."

THE END

The Great Street-car Robbery;

or,

The Newsboy Detective on the Trail

THE HAUNTED HOUSE ON DIVERSEY ST.
BANG! BANG!
WOLF PETE
"WHO ARE YOU?"

THE GREAT STREET-CAR ROBBERY; or THE NEWSBOY DETECTIVE ON THE TRAIL

Chapter 1

The Stranger

"ANOTHER trolley-car robbery! Aha! The city detectives are the veriest tyros!"

Such were the words spoken by a handsome youth, aged nine, as he stood on the corner and addressed his companions. Under his arm was a neat bundle of papers, bespeaking his occupation. He was none other than our old friend, Eddie Parks, the Newsboy Detective.

"Why do you not pursue an investigation of the case, that you may bring the guilty parties to justice?" asked Lawrence Hetherton, one of the most popular newsboys in Chicago.

"It may be advisable for me to do so," said our hero, meditatively. "The other detectives have failed in this case, and it is my duty to society to ferret out the perpetrators of these crimes."

At that moment a dark-haired man, with piercing eyes, passed the corner and gave a searching glance at the Newsboy Detective.

Our hero instinctively put his hand on his revolver.

"That person knows something about those robbers," said our hero, meaningly.

Who was the dark man?

Chapter 2

Who Was She?

ALL of the robberies which had startled the community had taken place in Sylvan Avenue.

The trolley cars traveling in Sylvan Avenue were patronized by residents of Rose Park, who were employed in stores situated in the heart of the city. It was no unusual thing for these passengers to carry from $1000 to $1500 each in money, to say nothing of jewelry, watches and precious stones. Therefore, it will be understood that the robbers had reaped a rich harvest.

The point usually selected for the attack on the car was in a dark grove in the 27th ward, miles from any human habitation.

One evening, shortly after the conversation related in our first chapter, a trolley car was speeding toward the dark woods mentioned above.

The passengers conversed gayly and the diamonds worn by the ladies were very beautiful.

There was no premonition of danger.

"Halt!"

This stern command was given by a masked man who stood on the track immediately in front of the car.

At the same instant three other men

emerged from the woods. They carried gleaming revolvers.

As the trolley car came to a stop, women screamed and brave men grew pale.

Surely it was enough to make the stoutest heart quail.

The robbers began to despoil the passengers of their valuables, thrusting into their pockets handfuls of glittering gems and great rolls of money.

"Come, give me your money and jewels," said a villain, who appeared to be the leader of the gang, addressing a beautiful young lady on the end seat.

"I will give you nothing, Edgar Black," was the scornful reply.

"Curse you! Who are you?"

"I will show you," said she, and with a swift movement the wig was removed.

It was the Newsboy Detective!

"Damnation!" shrieked Edgar Black.

The next instant our hero was engaged in a hand-to-hand encounter with four robbers.

Chapter 3

The Struggle

IT will be remembered that we left the Newsboy Detective engaged in a terrific combat with the four desperate highwaymen.

He fought with supreme strength, and at one time had three of the robbers lying prone on the earth. At the moment of victory he was struck heavily on the head from behind. He fell prone and lay unconscious.

His assailants retreated into the woods with shouts of triumph.

Recovering himself slowly, our hero looked about him. The trolley car was disappearing in the distance. All was silence around him.

Drawing a small vial from his pocket he touched his lips to a magic preparation which a friend had sent him from India. In a moment he was completely recovered.

Picking up his revolver, which had fallen

during the mêlée, he set off rapidly in the direction taken by the robbers.

Chapter 4

Darkness

OUR hero knew that by taking a few drops of the magic preparation occasionally he could run for hours without tiring and he was determined to keep on the trail of the miscreants who had robbed the trolley car.

Sure enough, after running for two hours across the desolate prairie, he was rewarded by the sight of a distant buggy containing the four men. He redoubled his speed and soon began to gain on the robbers.

Bang!

Bang!

Bang!

A volley of bullets whistled around him but he paid no heed. Lifting his six-shooter he began firing rapidly at the lines which guided the horses. One of them snapped and parted.

The horses, being no longer under control, swung to one side.

The four robbers were hurled through the air!

"At last!" shouted our hero.

At that moment he stumbled and fell forward.

A bullet had struck him in the head!

Chapter 5

The Cipher Message

WHEN our hero recovered consciousness it was broad daylight. It required some time for him to remember what had happened. An examination of the wound showed that the bullet had entered at the front of the forehead and had glanced along the skull, coming out at the back of the head.

Beyond a slight headache our hero suffered no inconvenience. A few drops of the magic preparation soon cured the headache.

As the Newsboy Detective arose to his feet he noticed that a piece of paper was pinned to his coat. It read as follows:

SO DIE ALL DETECTIVES!

"The robbers evidently thought they had finished me," said he, laughing cheerily; "but such is not the case."

Before departing our hero determined to make an examination of the scene. Near the place where he had fallen he found a card which had the following marks on it in red ink:

X + X + X + X + X + X + X

"This is evidently written in cipher," said he, examining the card with a thoughtful expression on his face.

For several minutes he studied the card and the cipher became clear to him. The reading on the card was as follows:

"All members of the gang will meet at the haunted house, corner of Plumsen Street and Diversey Avenue, Wednesday evening, at 8 o'clock sharp, in order to attend to the distribution of the swag. It is especially desired that the members will be on hand punctually, as there is much business to transact.

By order COMMITTEE."

"So far, so good," said our hero, putting the card into his pocket.

Chapter 6

The Haunted House

THE haunted house was a venerable structure, overgrown with vines and surrounded by tall trees.

The residents of that portion of the metropolis shunned it after nightfall, and it was, therefore, an ideal place for the robbers to assemble and divide their ill-gotten gains.

In an upper room, heavily curtained to prevent a ray of light escaping, sat Edgar

Black and two of his associates in crime. A black bottle was on the table, and the robbers took occasional long drafts of its contents.

"Is the swag safe?" asked one of the robbers, hoarsely.

"Safe as in the bank," replied Edgar Black, with a fearful leer. "There's nothin' to fear now, boys. The only one we was afraid of is out of the way."

"Yes, curse him; he's lying dead in the 27th ward," said another robber, "and it may be weeks or months before he is found. By that time we will be safely in Paris."

"Where's Wolf Pete?" asked Edgar Black, with an oath.

At that moment the door opened and the three robbers, looking up, recognized the familiar features of Wolf Pete, the most desperate member of the gang. He seated himself at the table and brusquely demanded an immediate division of the money and jewels.

Edgar Black went to the wall, and, touching a secret spring, opened a panel and brought forth a large tin box containing the proceeds of the car robbery. The box contained $37,000 in money and over $16,000 worth of watches and diamonds.

For several minutes not a word was spoken as the division was made. Each man put his fortune into a stout canvas bag. "Now, we're through," said Edgar Black, reaching for the black bottle.

"Not yet!" came in thunderous tones.

The door fell with a crash, and a dozen policemen in full uniform poured into the room!

Chapter 7

The Law

TRAPPED!" shouted Edgar Black, pale with rage.

"Yes; your time has come," replied the Chief of Police with a smile.

"Someone has betrayed me," exclaimed the leader, glaring at his companions.

"You are right, I did," replied Wolf Pete.

"You? Wolf Pete?"

"No; not Wolf Pete, but Eddie Parks, the Newsboy Detective," responded our hero, removing his disguise.

"Alive!" gasped Edgar Black.

"Yes; alive," said the Newsboy Detective; "and let me tell you this, Edgar Black, sooner or later every violator of the law will suffer direly."

"But where is Wolf Pete?" asked the Chief of Police.

"I intercepted him and borrowed his clothes," said our hero, with a quiet smile. "You will find him gagged and bound in the cellar."

"You are, indeed, a hero," said the Chief of Police.

Little remains to be told.

The robbers were promptly sent to prison, and our hero received $5000 reward which he generously gave to the widowed mother of Lawrence Hetherton.

THE END

The Klondike Rescue;

or,

The Mysterious Guide

STATE
$10,000!
SIXTY DEGREES BELOW!
BANG!
SAVED!
DEEP
MEDITATION

THE KLONDIKE RESCUE; or, THE MYSTERIOUS GUIDE

Chapter 1

The Stranger

"EXCUSE me, Miss."

Mae Watts stopped suddenly and looked in a startled manner at the stranger who had thus addressed her.

The scene we have just described took place in State Street in the great city of Chicago.

Mae Watts was indeed a beautiful girl. A complexion of alabaster whiteness contrasted with the ruby red of her lips. Her eyes were a liquid brown and when she smiled her teeth flashed in the sunlight.

"Have we met?" asked Miss Watts, with a questioning look at the stranger.

He was a handsome gentleman, with a

long mustache, silk hat, a satin-faced light overcoat with a red carnation in the button-hole, immaculate collar, neat blue cravat, gold watch chain, etc. In one of his gloved hands he carried a silver-headed cane.

"No, Miss, we have not met," said the strange gentleman in a voice of musical sweetness, causing a strange thrill to permeate Mae, "but I perceive that you are in trouble, and if I can be of any service to you I will do so."

Mae was now thoroughly reassured and spoke to the gentleman most confidentially.

"It is true that I am in trouble," she said, laying her hand on his arm. "My poor, dear father went to the Klondike late in August or early in September, I forgot which, and for weeks we have received no written communication from him."

"Would you have tidings of your father?" asked the stranger.

"I would," replied Miss Watts.

"Enough," said the stranger. "Here is money to provide for your immediate wants."

He pressed a roll of bills into her hand

and rapidly moved away toward the Northwestern Station.

Miss Watts counted the money.

He had left $10,000!

Chapter 2

AT SEA

MIDNIGHT on the Pacific!

The stark upper rigging swings black against the soft and opalescent clouds. The vessel rides the long and oily waves. Two lights move like slow pendulums at the yardarms. There is no sound save the occasional tugging of the sheet or the drawing of a timber.

A lonely man paces the deck. Apparently he is in deep meditation. Suddenly he pauses and says, half aloud: "Curse the luck! I forgot to inquire her father's name!"

Small difficulties seldom stand in the way of a man of determination. After pacing the deck for a half-hour or so, he retires to his cabin with a confident smile on his face.

He has laid his plans.

Chapter 3

Captured!

SIXTY degrees below zero!

A heavy layer of snow covered the gaunt hillsides of Alaska. So intense was the cold that even the pine trees were frozen stiff and did not bend before the boreal blasts that swept the icy ravines and lifted the sleet into blinding clouds.

Along the desolate trail, battling fiercely with the wind and moving slowly over the encrusted snow, came a solitary pedestrian, followed by two dogs hauling a sledge.

The traveler paused for a few minutes in the shelter of a huge bowlder.

"It is bitter cold," he said.

He had made the same observation more than 1300 times since leaving Dawson City.

"But I will not despair!" he added and for a moment a smile of anticipation showed on his frozen face. "On yonder sledge I have $800,000 worth of gold. Let me but live to get back to Chicago and I will take luncheon at the St. Hubert every day and

Mae shall wear violets while the other girls are wearing smilax."

Even as he spoke these hopeful words he chanced to raise his eyes and a groan of horror came from his lips.

Before him stood three Chilkoot Indians!

Chapter 4

The Nick of Time

As soon as Joseph H. Watts (for the solitary traveler was Mae's father, as the reader may have suspected) found himself in the hands of the Indians he gave up all hope.

He knew that if the Indians did not rob him outright they would either eat his provisions and leave him to starve or else insist on acting as his guides and charge the entire $800,000 for their services.

The unhappy traveler was not left in doubt. The Indians directed him to follow them. It was evident that they intended to lead him some distance from the trail and murder him.

Sure enough, they halted after a while and one of them said: "Gioo kaloo mahoo."

Joseph H. Watts had an imperfect knowledge of the Chilkoot language, but he knew that this meant: "Your time has come!"

Three rifles were pointed at Joseph H. Watts's heart.

He breathed a last prayer.

Suddenly the Indians dropped dead!

Chapter 5

The Rescuer

MR. WATTS was so astounded that he did not at first take cognizance of the approach of a stalwart figure clad in a full suit of fur. The man was heavily bearded, but he had a kindly eye.

"Another minute and I would have been too late," said the newcomer.

"What do you mean?" asked Mr. Watts. "Why did the Indians fall?"

"I shot them," was the terse reply.

"But I heard no report."

"That was because I used noiseless powder—a little invention of my own," and the rescuer laughed modestly.

"Then you have saved my life."

"I did my duty," said the other.

"Pray, whom have I to thank?" asked Mr. Watts, for he was a well-educated man. Otherwise he would have made a fortune in Chicago and would not have been compelled to brave the fearful hardships of a polar winter.

"Enough that I am a fellow citizen of the United States, the proudest country on which the sun shines."

Joseph H. Watts' eyes filled with tears.

At that moment a large bear appeared on top of a hill near by.

The rescuer pointed his weapon at the animal. There was no sound, but the bear gave a loud bellow and fell over in his tracks—dead.

The noiseless powder had done its work!

That evening the two Americans sat by a roaring camp fire, eating bear meat and singing "The Star-Spangled Banner."

Chapter 6

The Message

WHY need we tell of the many days of weary tramping along the trail before Joseph H. Watts and the rescuer reached Taiya?

The mysterious guide never told his name. Neither did he explain his presence in that lonely land. On the night of the arrival in Taiya he suddenly disappeared.

Mr. Watts sought everywhere for him, but was compelled to sail for home without seeing him again.

As the steamer was moving out to sea Mr. Watts felt a hand laid on his shoulder.

He turned and beheld a young man with auburn side whiskers, who gave him a note.

"From whom did it come?" asked Mr. Watts, always careful as to his grammar.

"I do not know," said the young man, with a significant smile.

Mr. Watts opened the note and read:

We shall meet again

Chapter 7

An Old Friend

LITTLE remains to be told.

Joseph H. Watts returned to Chicago, and, with $800,000 at his command, he took his place in refined society at once. Mae told him the story of the kind gentleman in State Street, and he oft repeated the tale of his rescue by the mysterious guide.

One day as Mae and her father were sitting on a divan in the Turkish room looking at the rugs, there was a ring at the doorbell, and the butler ushered into their presence a young man with auburn side whiskers.

Mr. Watts sprang toward him with an exclamation of joy.

"You are the young man I met on the ship coming from Alaska," said Mr. Watts.

"No," said the other, quickly removing his disguise, "*I am Eddie Parks, the Newsboy Detective!*"

"Then it was you—"

"It was I who rescued you from the Indians and guided you to Taiya."

"Why did you do this?"

"For your daughter's sake," replied our hero, blushing slightly.

"Then you are the kind gentleman I met on State Street?" exclaimed Mae.

"Yes!"

With a glad cry Mae rushed into his arms.

"You are an intrepid youth," said Mr. Watts, who was deeply affected. "You have done a noble service for me and my daughter. Come, I will share my fortune with you and you must make your home with us."

"No," said our hero, with great firmness. "I can not do so. I have my work to do. The weak must be protected. The wrongs of the innocent must be avenged."

Then, lifting his eyes heavenward, he recited:

"Right forever on the scaffold,
Wrong forever on the throne."

Mae wept silently.

THE END

The Goodlot Murder Case;

or,

Solving the Mystery

THE TRIAL
THE LEAP FOR LIFE!
"MAINTAIN QUIET!!"
McCUTCHEON

THE GOODLOT MURDER CASE; or, SOLVING THE MYSTERY

Chapter 1

"THE case is hopeless!"

So spoke the great criminal lawyer, and as he did so he sighed deeply.

"Tell me the facts again," said his companion, a proud-appearing youth of nine, as he took a notebook from his pocket.

"I will," said the other, dejectedly, "but I fear it can avail nothing. We can prove that Mrs. Goodlot has been missing since August 2nd. We know that she had quarreled with her husband, and that he had threatened her life. We can show that on the night of August 2nd, the defendant generated ozonotic gas in his chemical laboratory, and we have every reason to believe that he put his wife into the gas tank; but to prove it—ah, that is the difficulty!"

"What is the effect of ozonotic gas on human tissue?" asked the youth, with a thoughtful expression on his face.

"It converts all animal matter into gaseous vapor. Within ten minutes after the body had been put into the tank there was not a trace of solid substance left."

"I will examine that tank!"

"You!"

"Yes!"

"It is guarded constantly. They will kill you!"

"We shall see."

He arose, and after shaking hands with the great criminal lawyer, passed rapidly to a carriage in waiting. The reader may have suspected ere this that he was none other than Eddie Parks, the Newsboy Detective!

The Goodlot Murder

Chapter 2

The Night Encounter

"HALT!"

As this word was spoken a revolver gleamed in the moonlight.

The watchman standing at the great doorway of the Goodlot Chemical Laboratory strained his eyes to see what the object might be that was approaching.

"All right. Don't be afraid," came a gruff voice from the gloom, and a policeman stepped into view.

"I am glad it was you," said the watchman, in a relieved tone of voice. "We have instructions to shoot and kill any strangers found near the laboratory."

The next instant the watchman felt his throat clasped as if in a vise. He heard a voice at his ear: "Maintain quiet, or I will throttle you!"

In a few seconds he was bound and gagged. The policeman took the keys from the prostrate form.

"Now, my good man, stay here until I return," he said, chuckling. With that he threw off his disguise.

It was the Newsboy Detective!

Chapter 3

The Tower

BEFORE starting on his perilous night trip to the chemical laboratory our hero had studied a plan of the interior of the vast structure, so that, even in the pitch darkness it required but a few moments for him to find the tank in which the ozonotic gas had been generated.

Taking a can opener from his pocket, he cut a circular opening in the tank and crawled in.

After a few minutes he emerged with a satisfied smile on his face.

As he approached the doorway at which he had entered he saw four men standing in the moonlight. The other man on guard had discovered the bound and gagged watchman!

They were waiting for our hero to return!

"I will not be captured," he said, drawing his trusty revolver. At that moment his feet struck a bottle, which fell and broke with a crash!

The four men came through the doorway. Our hero turned and ran.

He knew that all the doorways were locked. His only hope was now the stairway!

The pursuers were close behind! Below he could hear the curses and ejaculations of the enraged watchman.

Suddenly he emerged into an open tower. He had reached the topmost point of the great building!

Over one hundred feet below he saw the placid river!

The pursuers came panting at his heels!

There was no time to be lost!

With a defiant shout he leaped far out from the tower and dived for the dark river!!

Chapter 4

On Hand Again

AT ten o'clock the next morning James H. Webster, the great criminal lawyer, was seated in his office.

He had waited for hours for tidings from our hero.

There was a knock at the door and Ralph Dumont, counsel for the defendant, entered the room.

"I came to tell you that the foolhardy youth who dared to visit the laboratory last night is no more," said he, a smile of triumph lighting up his malignant features.

"Dead!" exclaimed the great lawyer, blanching perceptibly.

"Yes—dead! He was pursued to the tower and leaped to the river. He did not come to the surface. So you see, Mr. Webster, that your trump card has failed. You can never convict Anthony Goodlot."

"Don't be too sure of that," came a quiet voice from behind.

"Perdition!" exclaimed Ralph Dumont.

Eddie Parks was standing in the doorway!

Chapter 5

The Tooth

AS soon as James H. Webster saw our hero alive and well he rushed toward him with open arms.

Ralph Dumont hurried from the room, muttering curses.

"He seems surprised to see me," said our hero, laughing merrily.

"You are indeed a brave youth," said the great lawyer, gazing at our hero in admiration. "But tell me, have you secured any evidence?"

"I have," replied our hero, modestly and taking a small paper from his pocket he unrolled it and showed a false tooth.

"This is a porcelain tooth, and was not affected by the gas," said he. "After finding this tooth I inquired the name of Mrs. Goodlot's dentist."

"Aha!" said the great lawyer.

"I looked up the address in the directory, and upon going to the address I learned that the dentist died three years ago."

"Curse the luck!" exclaimed James H. Webster. "The fates are against us. Is there no one else who can identify this tooth?"

"There is a way," said our hero. "Leave it to me. Now let us deposit the tooth in a place of safety."

As they passed out of the building there was a terrific explosion and James H. Webster's office was completely wrecked.

Chapter 6

The Trial

THE Goodlot murder trial was in progress.

The prosecution was about to close its side of the case.

There had been no direct testimony to show that Anthony Goodlot had murdered his wife.

The attorneys for the defense were jubilant.

Ralph Dumont smiled sneeringly at James H. Webster.

"Edward Parks!"

At the call of this name there was a sensation, for the fame of the Newsboy Detective had spread far and wide.

Our hero modestly stepped to the witness chair and faced the hushed assemblage.

After the usual preliminaries, James H. Webster handed him a small box containing the porcelain tooth.

"Do you recognize the article in that box," was asked.

"I do," replied our hero.

"What is it?"

"It is a false tooth made of porcelain."

"State whether or not you ever saw this tooth before."

"I found this tooth in the gas tank in the Goodlot factory on the night of September 23rd."

Our hero briefly related the circumstances under which he had found the tooth.

"Do you know what person, if any, had

ever used that tooth?" asked the lawyer.

"I found that the person who used that tooth and the person who chewed the gum contained in this box are one and the same."

With these words our hero drew a paper box from his pocket.

"What does the box contain?" asked James H. Webster.

"It contains 423 pieces of chewed gum, each piece showing the imprint of human teeth."

"You may state where you found that gum."

"At the residence of Anthony Goodlot, stuck along the under edges of chairs, tables, shelves, piano, piano stool, mantels, desks, whatnots, folding beds, railings, banisters, sofas, and bookcases. I found twenty-two portions of chewed gum stuck on the columns of the front veranda and I found fourteen on various chandeliers and brackets. I found three on one closet door and two on the caster in the pantry."

"Have you attempted to fit the porcelain

tooth, which you found in the gas tank, into any of the imprints or indentations on any of these 423 pieces of chewed gum?"

"I have."

"Tell the court what, if anything, you have learned."

"The porcelain tooth fits into the deepest mark on every one of the 423 pieces."

Ralph Dumont arose to cross-examine the witness.

He trembled violently and his face was purple with rage. When he attempted to speak he gave vent to incoherent sounds and fell to the floor in an apoplectic fit!

Chapter 7

Justice

AS soon as our hero had finished his testimony, the prosecution called other witnesses to prove that Mrs. Goodlot had a false tooth and that she was the only one around the house who chewed gum.

Little remains to be told.

Our hero was again recognized as the greatest detective of the age.

The defense could not shatter his testimony in regard to the tooth.

Without leaving their seats, the jurors brought in a verdict of "justifiable homicide."

THE END

The Avenger and General Bolero;

or,

The Spanish Plot Foiled

MORRO CASTLE
CARRAMBA!
BANG!
THE ESCAPE

THE AVENGER AND GENERAL BOLERO; or,

THE SPANISH PLOT FOILED

Chapter 1

In the Darkness

IN a remote street of the great west division of Chicago there stands a tall gloomy building. This building was once used as a factory. On this night in December it was supposed to be unoccupied. Not so.

Seven men sat huddled together in one of the rooms on the second floor. A lighted candle stood on the table. The men were heavily muffled, for the night was cold. They talked in whispers.

"Will he come?" asked one.

"I am sure of it," said another.

Both men spoke with a foreign accent.

Suddenly there was a rap at the door.

Bang! Bang!

One of the seven stealthily opened the door and had a whispered conversation with some one standing outside in the darkness.

"He will not come in until the candle is extinguished," said the man at the door.

After a short consultation, the light was snuffed out and in the pitch darkness a voice said: "I have come to tell you that I will rescue General Bolero from the Matanzas prison."

"Who are you?" asked one of the seven.

"You may speak of me as 'The Avenger.' "

"Why do you refuse to show your face?"

"Because you have in your band a traitor. He pretends to be a Cuban patriot, but in reality he is a spy in the employ of Spain."

Bang! went a revolver.

There was a hurry of footsteps. A light was struck.

Six men stood in the room! "The Avenger" had gone. So had Rico Portico!

Was he a spy?

Chapter 2

The Conspirator

SOME ten days later a beautiful vessel swept by the frowning Morro Castle and came to anchor in the magnificent harbor of Havana.

Almost immediately a small boat put out from shore and rapidly approached the vessel. In the stern sat Major Claro of the Spanish Army, a large and handsome man of dignified bearing.

As he stepped on the deck of the vessel he was met by a young man attired in the uniform of a Spanish captain. The young man had a coal-black mustache, raven hair and keen, restless eyes.

"Major Claro?"

"Yes, sir."

"I am Captain Rico Portico, and I have just returned from a secret mission to Chicago. I have discovered a conspiracy to liberate General Bolero. One of the conspirators is aboard."

"Aha!"

"Yon man who watches me so closely is the one you seek."

Major Claro stepped up to the swarthy young man indicated and said:

"You are my prisoner."

"Prisoner!" exclaimed the young man. "Surely you do not mean it. I am a loyal Spanish subject."

"Let me see your passports."

The young man put his hand into his pocket and then said, in apparent dismay: "Why, they're gone! They've been stolen!"

"A likely story," said Major Claro, mockingly.

At a signal four soldiers seized the young man and hurried him away.

He was doomed to a dungeon in Morro Castle!

Chapter 3

Plotting the Ambush

THAT evening Major Claro and Captain Rico Portico sat in a café overlooking the Plaza Pazaza and had a long conversation over their coffee and cigarros.

"You have rendered a valuable service, Captain Portico," said the Major. "Pray how did you learn of the conspiracy?"

"While I was in Chicago I posed as a Cuban patriot and became one of the leaders of the junta," replied the Captain. "As soon as I heard of the conspiracy to liberate General Bolero, I notified General Blanco. Then I followed the agent of the conspirators to New York and embarked on the same vessel."

"The plot has been entirely baffled," said the Major.

"Listen!" continued the Captain. "General Bolero knows that there is to be an effort to release him. Let him continue to think so. Do not permit your prisoner in Morro Castle to communicate with anyone. I will go to the Matanzas Prison and represent myself to Bolero as the agent of the conspirators. I will tell him that I have bribed the guards and provided for his escape. He shall be given into my custody, on order of General Blanco, and then as he rides away from the prison he can be shot by your soldiers in ambush. Thus the government can rid itself of a dangerous character and at the same time escape the charge of assassination."

"Wonderful!" ejaculated the Major. "Do you think your plan will succeed?"

A strange glitter came into the eyes of Captain Portico as he replied:

"I will succeed or die!"

Chapter 4

The Escape

IT was midnight.

The moonlight flooded the dreary walls of Matanzas Prison. There was no sound except the measured tread of the guard.

Stretching away eastward and westward from the prison lay a broad level road, showing white in the moonlight. A quarter of a mile to the east a company of soldiers waited, hidden in the high vegetation.

Their horses were secreted farther back from the roadway.

It was the ambush waiting to fire on General Bolero!

While the soldiers waited in silence, a whispered consultation was being held in General Bolero's little cell at the prison.

"May I trust you?" he asked, taking the hand of Captain Portico.

"I swear that I will either deliver you to your friends or die by your side."

"Then I will go."

"Good! The guards will allow us to pass. I have two horses waiting at the gate."

A few moments later the two men breathed the cool night air. The servant led two horses from a dark shed.

Captain Portico leaped to the saddle and General Bolero followed example.

"Follow me," said the captain, tersely.

He turned his horse's head—*not to the east, but to the west!*

Away they flew!

Chapter 5

The Pursuit

WITHIN ten minutes after General Bolero and his companion dashed away from the prison gate the soldiers in ambush learned of the trick that had been played on them.

Immediately they started in pursuit of the escaped prisoner and the traitorous Captain Portico.

All night they rode like mad, and at daybreak they sighted the two horsemen and bore down upon them.

"We are lost!" exclaimed General Bolero to his companion.

"Not so," said the younger man, with an easy smile.

He drew from his pocket a few dynamite cartridges and tossed them in the roadway pavement.

"Wait until one of those cartridges is struck by a horse's hoof," he said, glancing back at the pursuers.

Hardly had he spoken when there was a

fearful explosion and the squad of cavalry was blown to atoms!

Chapter 6

The Disguise

AFTER being rid of their pursuers the two horsemen went at a more leisurely pace.

"I owe my life to you, Captain Portico," said General Bolero.

"I am not Rico Portico," replied his companion, with a significant smile. "Rico Portico lies in Morro Castle, a prisoner. When I discovered him on the ship I knew that he was watching me. I stole his passports, assumed the disguise of a Spanish captain and denounced him as the real conspirator. After he was placed in Morro Castle I had Major Claro issue an order to prevent his communicating with anyone outside the prison. If he could have sent a message to General Blanco he would have thwarted my plan for your escape."

"Wonderful! Then you are not a Cuban?"

"I am an American," said the other, proudly.

"But you speak perfect Spanish."

"I learned it at night school in Chicago."

Chapter 7

FINALE

LITTLE remains to be told.

The mysterious rescuer who had assumed the name of Rico Portico, and who was known to the Cuban junta as "The Avenger," was welcomed as a hero when he returned to the land of the free and the home of the brave.

His name was on every tongue.

The President of the United States sent for him promptly and congratulated him handsomely.

Standing in a spacious apartment at the White House, our hero listened modestly to the words of praise spoken by him who holds the highest office within the gift of a free people.

"Men call you 'The Avenger,' " said the President. "Surely you have some other name."

"Yes," said our hero, quietly, as he removed his disguise.

The President was astounded.

Before him stood Eddie Parks, the Newsboy Detective!

THE END